SOLITA AND THE PURPLE MOON
A Children's Book

SOLITA Y LA LUNA MORADA
Un Libro Para Niños

Written in dual language: English and Spanish by Miriam Isabel Elliott

Illustrated by: Carlos E. Elliott

AuthorHouse™
1663 Liberty Drive
Bloomington, IN 47403
www.authorhouse.com
Phone: 833-262-8899

Because of the dynamic nature of the Internet, any web addresses or links contained in this book may have changed since publication and may no longer be valid. The views expressed in this work are solely those of the author and do not necessarily reflect the views of the publisher, and the publisher hereby disclaims any responsibility for them.

This book is printed on acid-free paper.

ISBN: 978-1-4343-4932-3 (sc)
ISBN: 978-1-4634-6453-0 (e)

Print information available on the last page.

Published by AuthorHouse 07/06/2021

Inspired by Madison Isabella.
This story is dedicated to her and to all the children
of our men and women in uniform serving our country.

Inspirado por Madison Isabella.
Este cuento es dedicado a ella y a todos los hijos
de los hombres y mujeres en uniforme que sirven a nuestro País.

A little girl lays on her bed at night…
She feels lonely and scared.
A cloud passes in front of her window and says hello.
Behind the cloud, a purple moon smiles,
coming closer and touching the glass.

"Knock, knock little girl. I am your friend,
I will come to you at bedtime every night.
Look at me; I am your favorite color!
I do it for you to bring you comfort."

"Oh, Purple Moon, stay, stay,
until I fall asleep and it is day again!"

And Purple Moon stayed.

Una niñita estaba acostada sobre su cama sintiéndose sola y asustada,
una nube que pasaba por su ventana la saluda. Detrás de la nube,
una luna morada se asoma y tocando en el vidrio le sonríe.
"Tun, Tun niñita, soy tu amiga, vendré a ti por las noches, mírame bien.
¡Soy tu color favorito, te traigo alegría!"
"¡Oh, Luna Morada, quédate hasta que yo me duerma y sea mañana!"

Y Luna Morada la acompañó.

Many nights went by and the moon always came
to knock on the window of the lonely little girl
who waited in the darkness of her room by the bed.

"Knock, knock, little girl, here I am:
as purple as I can be and ready to play!
I will change my round shape to make you smile.
I will be a square, a triangle, a kite—
or I will bring you playmates from the sky,
to dance by your window all night, all night."

"Oh, Purple Moon, I love you. Stay and be my friend.
Hold on to my window until it is day again!"

And Purple Moon stayed.

Muchas noches pasaron y la luna siempre llegaba a tocar en la
ventana de la niñita quien esperaba en la oscuridad de su cuarto.

"¡Tun, Tun niñita, aquí estoy, muy morada y lista para hacerte reír!
Seré un triangulo, un cometa o me pondré cuadrada,
pero si prefieres te traeré estrellas para que bailen en tu ventana
toda la noche, toda la noche."

"¡Oh, Luna Morada, te quiero, quédate y sé mi amiga. Agárrate de mi ventana
hasta que llegue el día!"

Y la Luna Morada la acompañó.

One dark windy night, the moon did not show
by the little girl's window at all.
She sat on the floor of her room and cried
many hours into the night.
She fell asleep holding a book
her mommy read to her
slowly, slowly, before she left,
with the sweetest voice Solita ever heard.
She called her mommy and she called the moon...
but that night, no one came,
and Solita slept and slept until it was day again.

*Una noche oscura y ventosa la luna no apareció por la ventana de la niñita,
quien se sentó en el suelo a llorar, abrazada a un libro que su madre
le había leído antes de partir, despacito con voz dulce y amorosa.
Esa noche, la niñita llamaba a su madre y llamaba a la luna,
pero no vinieron. Entonces entre sollozos se durmió hasta que
amaneció.*

The next night, Solita ran to her room.
It was dark, and there was no wind.
She got on her bed, looking outside,
waiting for her friend in the lonely night,
until a purple light illuminated her window.

"Knock, knock, little girl, I am here again
to play with you, to become any shape!
Last night I was not able to come on time,
but earlier this morning, I held your hand,
and with your tears, I made you a star
to put in your hair tonight."

"Oh, Purple Moon, stay, stay!
You are my best friend!
Hold on to my window until it is day."

And Purple Moon stayed.

A la noche siguiente Solita corrió a su cuarto. Estaba oscuro y sin viento.
Sentadita sobre su cama miraba hacia afuera, esperando a su amiga.
Hasta que un resplandor morado apareció en su ventana.

"¡Tun, tun niñita, aquí estoy! ¡Vengo a jugar contigo y me convertiré
en la forma que desees! Anoche no pude llegar a tiempo, pero esta mañana
de tus lagrimitas te hice una estrella para adornar tu pelo.-
"¡Oh, Luna Morada, quédate! ¡Eres mi mejor amiga! Agárrate de mi ventana
hasta que llegue el día."

Y Luna Morada la acompañó.

The months were passing by,
and the moon always came
to visit Solita and be her friend;
to watch her color her room with dreams
of Mommy returning to kiss her and read
her favorite book, slowly and sweet.

"Oh, Purple Moon, you look so cute today!
Where is the other half of you?
Is that a new game? I would like to play!"

"Hop in, little girl, I will give you a ride:
across this land, across the sky!
Hold on to me, let's have fun!
We will return to your room later on.
Let's fly, Solita, hold on!"

Los meses fueron pasando, y la Luna siempre llegaba a visitar a Solita
y ser su amiga. La veía colorear su cuarto con sueños de su Mama regresando
a casa, dándole besos y leyéndole su libro favorito, dulcemente y muy despacito.
"Oh, Luna Morada, te ves tan simpática hoy. ¿Dónde has dejado tu otra mitad?
Si esto es un juego nuevo.¡Yo quiero jugar!"
"¡Súbete niñita! Te daré un paseo a través de esta tierra, a través del cielo.
Aférrate de mí, nos divertiremos.
¡Sujétate fuertemente, Solita, volaremos!"

They flew around and around and around
the blue sky and over the sea.
They saw and they saw
mountains, rivers, lakes
and gigantic trees with long arms,
and magical leaves
singing songs to the night: singing songs
of love to America, the land of the free.

"Hold on Solita, hold on.
Let's travel faster and faster,
touch the clouds, tomorrow is almost here.
Let's get back now, your happiness is near!"

"Oh, Purple Moon, take me home, I am tired."

And Purple Moon took her home.

Niñita y Luna volaron a través del cielo y sobre el mar. Vieron montes,
ríos, lagos y árboles gigantescos de brazos largos y hojas mágicas
cantando canciones de amor a América, la hermosa.

"¡Agárrate Solita, agárrate! ¡Viajemos rápido, toca las nubes! Que es casi mañana.
¡La felicidad se acerca a tu casa, volvamos!"

"Oh, Luna Morada, llévame a mi cama que estoy cansada."

Y Luna Morada la complació.

Tired from her travels with her best friend,
over the sea and across the land,
the little girl slept and slept,
day and night, night and day,
holding her favorite book close to her chest.

Slowly, slowly, her room door opened...
a silhouette came and sat by her bed.
Taking the book in her hands, she read
with the sweetest voice Solita ever heard.
Slowly, slowly, she read and she read,
until the little girl opened her eyes and said:

"Oh, Mommy, you are back! Stay, stay,
until I grow up and be like you.
Oh, Mommy, I love you, stay, stay!"

...And a little star told me that mother and child
waved to the moon while it faded away,
to visit other windows of scared and lonely children,
not too far from them.

Agotada de su viaje con la Luna sobre el mar y a través de la tierra,
la niñita durmió y durmió. Día y noche, noche y día abrazada a su libro
favorito.

Despacito la puerta de su cuarto se abrió. Una silueta se sentó
al borde de la cama, y tomando el libro comenzó a leer con voz suave.
Despacio y dulcemente leyó y leyó hasta que Solita abrió los ojos exclamando:

"¡Oh, Mama volviste! ¡Quédate, quédate conmigo hasta que yo crezca!
¡Te quiero Mama, quédate!"

...Y me contaba una estrellita, que madre e hija se despidieron de la luna,
mientras que se perdía entre las nubes, rumbo a otras ventanas de niños
asustados y solitarios que no estaban muy lejos.